Play Ball!

Dona Herweck Rice

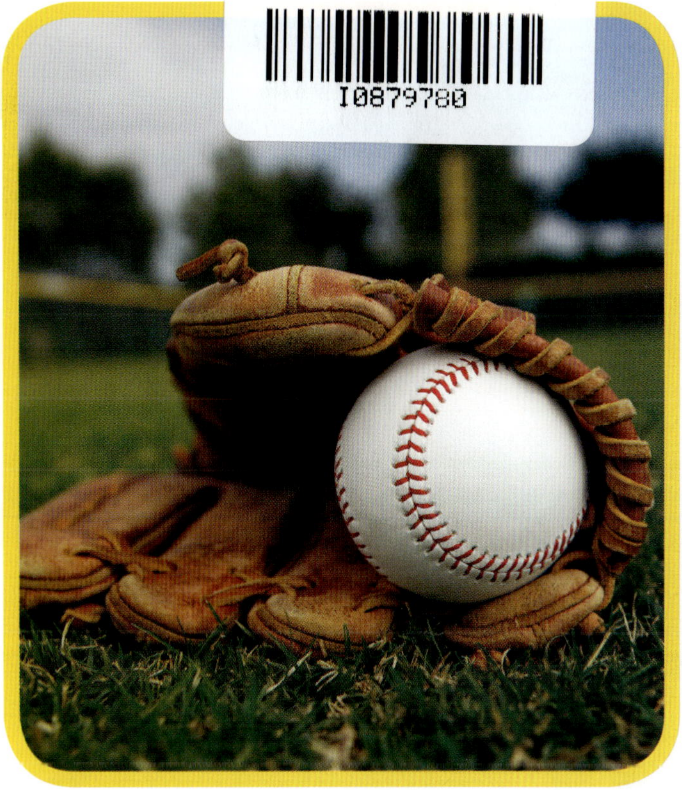

Publishing Credits

Rachelle Cracchiolo, M.S.Ed., *Publisher*
Conni Medina, M.A.Ed., *Managing Editor*
Nika Fabienke, Ed.D., *Content Director*
Véronique Bos, *Creative Director*
Shaun N. Bernadou, *Art Director*
Carol Huey-Gatewood, M.A.Ed., *Editor*
Valerie Morales, *Associate Editor*
Courtney Roberson, *Senior Graphic Designer*

Image Credits: All images from iStock and/or Shutterstock.

Teacher Created Materials
5301 Oceanus Drive
Huntington Beach, CA 92649-1030
www.tcmpub.com

ISBN 978-1-4938-9830-5

© 2019 Teacher Created Materials, Inc.

Printed in Malaysia. Thumbprints.45293

I0879780

He  his  .

sees bat

He 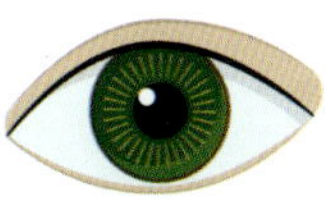 his  .

sees ball

He 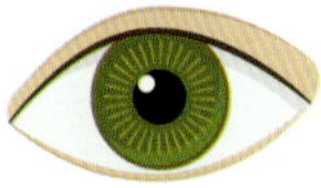 his 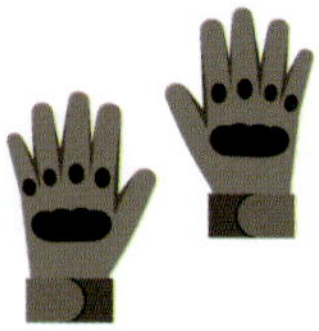 .

sees gloves

He 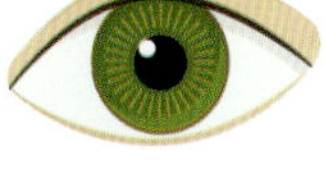 his  .

sees mitt

He 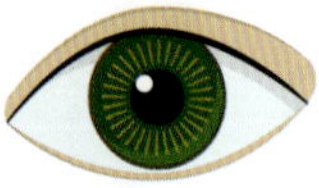 his .

sees cap

He 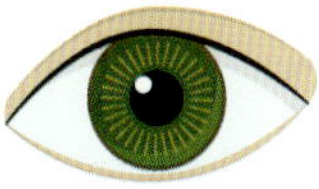 his  .

sees helmet

He 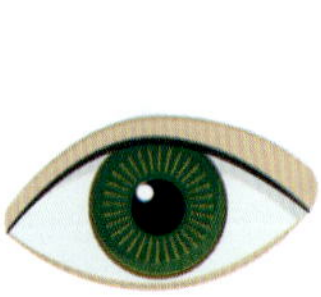 his  .

sees water bottle

He 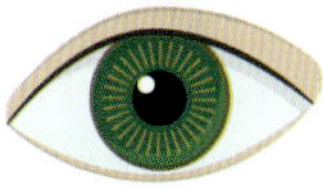 his  .

sees bag

He  his  .

sees team

He 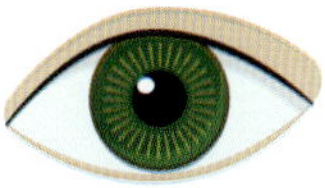 his  .

sees trophy

High-Frequency Words

he
his